First published in 2006
by Meadowside Children's Books
185 Fleet Street, London, EC4A 2HS
Illustrations © Jacqueline East 2006

The right of Jacqueline East to be identified
as the illustrator of this work has been
asserted by her in accordance with the Copyright,
Designs and Patents Act, 1988

A CIP catalogue record for this book
is available from the British Library
Printed in China

ISBN 10 pbk 1-84539-151-9
ISBN 13 pbk 978-1-84539-151-5

ISBN 10 hbk 1-84539-152-7
ISBN 13 hbk 978-1-84539-152-2

10 9 8 7 6 5 4 3 2

Cuddle!

Written by
Beth Shoshan

Illustrated by
Jacqueline East

meadowside 🍃
CHILDREN'S BOOKS

I'd cuddle a whale,
but I might be
too small,

I'd cuddle
a giraffe,
but I think
he's too tall.

I'd cuddle
a hedgehog
but, ouch!,
they're so spiky,

I'd cuddle a crocodile.

If I cuddled
a gorilla

I'd cuddle a skunk
but I think they're
too smelly,

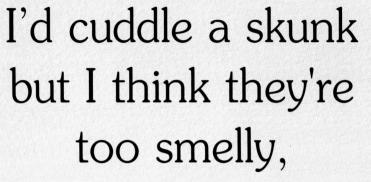

I'd cuddle a shark

but I'd be in his belly!

I'd cuddle
a python

way up high
in a tree

I'd cuddle
a hippo
who might just
squash me.

I'd cuddle a lion

but he'd bite off my head,

Do you think
I can cuddle
my Teddy
instead?

For Uncle John
&
Aunty Sheila

J.E.